Other books by Helen Morgan

MARY KATE AND THE SCHOOL BUS
MEET MARY KATE
SATCHKIN PATCHKIN

Helen Morgan

Mary Kate and the

Jumble Bear

and other stories

Illustrated by Shirley Hughes

Puffin Books

PUFFIN BOOKS

Published by the Penguin Group
Penguin Books Ltd, 27 Wrights Lane, London W8 5TZ, England
Penguin Books USA Inc., 375 Hudson Street, New York, New York 10014, USA
Penguin Books Australia Ltd, Ringwood, Victoria, Australia
Penguin Books Canada Ltd, 10 Alcorn Avenue, Toronto, Ontario, Canada M4V 3B2
Penguin Books (NZ) Ltd, 182–190 Wairau Road, Auckland 10, New Zealand

Penguin Books Ltd, Registered Offices: Harmondsworth, Middlesex, England

First published by Faber and Faber Ltd, 1967
Published in Puffin Books 1982
10 9 8 7 6 5 4

Copyright © Helen Morgan, 1967
Illustrations copyright © Faber and Faber Ltd, 1967
All rights reserved

Printed in England by Clays Ltd, St Ives plc
Set in VIP Baskerville

For the little children of Bowling Green School

Contents

The Jumble Bear

Teddy was lost. When Mary Kate woke up one morning he wasn't in the bed with her. She felt under the pillow but there wasn't anything there except a screwed-up blue handkerchief with little white dots on it.

'I'm *sure* I brought Teddy to bed last night,' she said to herself. She lifted up the bedclothes and looked into the dark cave they made, but there wasn't anything there except her own two legs in screwed-up pink pyjamas.

Mary Kate scrambled out of bed and looked all round the room, but she couldn't see him. There was Og, the golly, on the window-sill with Black Bobo and Ben-Bun, the floppy rabbit, but Teddy wasn't with them. Nor was he on the cupboard by the bed, with Quackety Duck and Wooldog, the knitted puppy Auntie Dot had made for her.

'He must be downstairs in the pram with Dorabella,' thought Mary Kate and went down to the hall to look.

Teddy wasn't in the pram. Nor was Dorabella. She was sitting on the hall table in her hat and coat, waiting to be taken out. Mary Kate put her into the pram and told her to go to sleep and then crept back up the stairs. It was so quiet down in the hall that she knew Mummy and Daddy couldn't be up yet.

Up in her bedroom, Mary Kate opened the door of her new blue wardrobe to see if Teddy was in there on the shelf with the shoes. He wasn't. She looked in the drawers of the dressing-table to see if he was hiding under her clothes, but he wasn't. By this time she was beginning to feel a bit cross.

'Where *is* he?' she said to Og and Black Bobo. They just stared at her. They didn't know where Teddy was, either.

Mary Kate sat down on the Stripy Tiger rug that Granny had made her and pulled all the things out of the cupboard by the bed. She found several other things she thought she had lost but she didn't find Teddy. She was halfway through pushing the

10

things back into the cupboard when she thought of another place to look.

'Under the bed!' she said to herself and lay down on the Stripy Tiger himself and wriggled under the edge of the counterpane into the dark.

Just then, Mummy came in to say 'Good morning'. She didn't say it, though, because Mary Kate wasn't there. At least, Mummy thought she wasn't there, but as she turned to go out of the room she saw one of Mary Kate's legs poking out from under the bed.

11

'Whatever are you doing down there?' asked Mummy, stooping to pick her up.

'Looking for Teddy,' Mary Kate told her. 'He's lost.'

'He can't be *lost*,' said Mummy, putting Mary Kate into her dressing-gown. 'Just mislaid. We'll find him presently. You'd better come down and have breakfast with Daddy this morning, since you're so wide awake.'

So Mary Kate went downstairs behind Mummy and had breakfast with Daddy, like Saturdays and Sundays. Daddy cut her toast into fingers for her and gave her some of his special marmalade which had big pieces of orange peel in it and wasn't quite as sweet as the marmalade Mummy and Mary Kate usually had. Mary Kate liked it, though she did have to chew hard because of the peel.

By the time Daddy had gone to catch his train and Mary Kate was washed and dressed, she had quite forgotten about Teddy.

'We must dash round this morning,' Mummy said, when the breakfast things were washed up. 'Mrs Sharpe is coming at eleven o'clock to collect the things for the Jumble Stall at the Fête on Saturday. I still have one or two more things to sort out before she comes.'

'Shall I sort out something, too?' asked Mary Kate, not quite sure what a Jumble Stall was.

'Well...' said Mummy, thoughtfully. 'If you've anything you don't want that isn't broken or dirty I daresay Mrs Sharpe will take it. They usually have a Toy Corner on the stall. Come upstairs and look through your cupboard while I make the beds.'

Mary Kate didn't say she already *had* looked through her cupboard once that morning! She didn't say what a mess it was in, either. She just followed Mummy up the stairs and went into her bedroom to look through her toys while Mummy went into *her* bedroom to make her bed.

'Did you find anything?' asked Mummy, coming in a few minutes later to find Mary Kate sitting on the floor surrounded by toys.

'Yes,' said Mary Kate, holding up a red and green striped ball. 'This ball. I had two, just the same. One from Uncle Ned and one from Granny. And there are two Red Indians and an engine without any trucks. Will they do?'

'I'm sure they will,' smiled Mummy, beginning to put Mary Kate's toys back into the cupboard. 'There's a big cardboard box in my room. You go and put your jumble into it with mine while I tidy up in here and make your bed.'

Off went Mary Kate with the two Red Indians

13

and the ball and the engine without any trucks. She found the box by Mummy's bed and put the things into it. It was half full of jumble already. Mary Kate thought she would look and see what Mummy had found for the Fête.

She was just trying to open an interesting-looking wooden box when Mummy came into the room. She had something in her hand. It was Teddy!

'Where did you find him?' asked Mary Kate, taking him and looking at him to make quite sure he was still the same.

'Right at the bottom of your bed,' Mummy said. 'All tucked up with the blankets. You must have kicked him down there in the night.'

'I didn't,' said Mary Kate. 'He kicked himself down there. He's naughty. He was hiding to make me hunt and hunt for him. Naughty Teddy!'

She threw him across the room to punish him. She threw him hard, to let him know how cross she was. She threw him so hard that he went out through the open window!

'That was a silly thing to do, wasn't it?' said Mummy, going to the window to look out. Mary Kate followed her. There was a greengrocer's van going down the hill and a motor bike coming up and a bus just passing the house.

14

'I hope Teddy didn't go into the road,' Mary Kate said. 'The bus will run right over him if he did.'

Mary Kate's house was very near the road. It didn't really have a front garden, only a little sloping bank that Daddy had made into a rockery. Beyond that was the footpath, which was very narrow, and then the busy road.

'*Is* he in the road?' Mary Kate asked anxiously, when the bus had gone by.

Mummy leaned out to look. 'I can't see him anywhere,' she said. 'I'll go down and look properly.'

Mary Kate stayed where she was. She was never allowed to go in front of the house by herself in case she fell.

Mummy came round the side of the house and down the three steps to the front gate. At the same moment Mrs Sharpe appeared on the footpath. She had come out of the driveway. Mary Kate could just see the back of her little red car behind the big lilac bush.

Mummy came back into the bedroom. 'Mrs Sharpe's in a hurry,' she said, picking up the big box of jumble. 'I'll find Teddy when she's gone.'

She didn't find him, though. She hunted among the plants on the rockery and in the lavender clump and along the footpath and in the road, but Teddy wasn't there. When Daddy came home Mummy told him all about it and he hunted, too. He even shook the big lilac bush but he didn't find Teddy.

'Someone must have come along and picked him up while you were talking to Mrs Sharpe,' he said.

'I suppose so,' sighed Mummy. 'We were all in the hall going through the jumble and the front door was shut.'

'You'd better put a card on the board in the Post Office,' Daddy suggested, 'and I'll ask Jack Turner if anyone's handed Teddy in to him.'

Mr Turner was the policeman. He lived in a neat little house with a dark blue door at the other end of the village. No one had taken Teddy to his house, though. No one took Teddy to the Post Office, either, in spite of the card with big writing on it that Mummy put on the board.

Daddy called at Mr Turner's again on the way to the Fête on Saturday afternoon. It was no use. Teddy wasn't there.

'We'll see if we can find you something nice at the Fête,' Mummy said and she took Mary Kate to the Gift Stall. Mary Kate looked at all the pretty things but she didn't see anything she wanted.

'Try the Jumble Stall,' suggested Daddy, so they did.

'Toys over there!' called Mrs Sharpe from behind a pile of cardigans and pullovers. 'You're early, so you'll have first pick!'

Mary Kate went to the end of the stall. There was her red and green ball and there were the two

Indians, standing on the front of the engine without any trucks. Behind them was a pile of books and sitting on top of the pile was ... what do you think? Teddy! Really and truly Mary Kate's own Teddy, in his red trousers and blue jacket with the button missing!

'I found him in one of the boxes on the roof-rack,' Mrs Sharpe said, when they asked her about it. 'I must have been passing the window to turn into your driveway when Mary Kate threw him out.'

'I'll never throw him out again,' Mary Kate said, hugging her Jumble Bear. 'I don't care *how* naughty he is!'

Cake and
Aunt Mary

Mary Kate had a cold. Her head was muzzy
and her ears were buzzy and her nose was no
use at all. She went to bed in the middle of
the afternoon and didn't want any tea.

In the night she cried, because her ear was hurt-
ing. Mummy gave her a little pill and a cool drink
and put a piece of warmed cotton-wool in her ear.
Daddy held a square of flannel in front of the electric
fire till it was really warm and then put it on the
pillow under Mary Kate's head. It was lovely and
cosy and the ache in her ear soon went away.

The next morning the doctor came to see her. He
looked into her ear with a funny torch thing. It was
cold and it tickled. He held his watch up for Mary
Kate to listen to, but she couldn't hear it ticking.

'You've got to go to the hospital and see a

specialist,' Mummy said, when she came back into the bedroom after seeing the doctor out. 'Doctor's going to arrange it as soon as you're over this cold.'

So when Mary Kate's cold was quite gone, Mummy took her to the hospital. Granny went with them. So did Teddy. Mary Kate said he wanted to ride in a bus.

The specialist's name was Mr Smiley. 'Hallo, Princess,' he said, when Mary Kate went into the room. He held her hand and talked to her for a bit and then he looked at her ears and her nose and her throat. Then he said she would have to have her adenoids out, because they were too big.

'Come and see me the week after next,' he said. 'On Thursday. Bring Teddy with you, if you like.'

'Let's go and have a peep at the ward,' Granny said, when they came out of Mr Smiley's room. 'Then Mary Kate can see where she'll be coming.'

'And Teddy,' said Mary Kate. 'He's coming, too.'

They went up in the lift to the ward where Mary Kate was going to be. It had nine beds in it and it was quite empty! There was a rocking-horse in the middle of the floor.

'Can I ride on it?' asked Mary Kate.

'Not today,' said Mummy. 'Wait till you come and stay here.'

A nurse in a pink uniform came out of a wash-room.

'Haven't you any patients?' asked Granny.

'Not today,' said the nurse. 'They don't stay long in this ward, you know. We do sometimes have one left over till Tuesday, but we're nearly always empty on a Wednesday. We shall have some more tomorrow.'

She looked at Mary Kate and Teddy. 'Are you coming tomorrow?' she asked.

'No,' said Mary Kate. 'I'm coming the week after next.'

'I'll look out for you, then,' said the nurse.

'I like that pink nurse,' Mary Kate said as she followed Mummy and Granny back to the lift.

The week after next soon came. Mary Kate was up early on the Thursday morning. She came down the stairs before Daddy had finished his breakfast. He gave her a piece of toast.

'You needn't have got up yet,' he said. 'You don't have to go to the hospital till this afternoon, you know.'

'I've got a lot to do,' said Mary Kate. 'I have to put all my children to bed before I go. You will look after them, won't you, Daddy?'

'Of course,' promised Daddy.

In the middle of the morning Aunt Mary

21

arrived. 'I couldn't let my one and only niece go into hospital without coming to make sure they gave her a comfortable bed,' she said, giving Mary Kate a little parcel.

Inside the parcel was a pair of red slippers with little golden bows on the toes. 'Granny sent them,' Aunt Mary said. 'I called to see her on my way here. She's coming to the bus stop to see us off.'

'Put the slippers in the basket with your dressing-gown,' Mummy said. 'Take your old ones out first, though. And don't forget to remind me to buy you a new toothbrush when we go out.'

Granny was already waiting at the bus stop when Mummy and Aunt Mary and Mary Kate came out of the churchyard. They had taken the short cut because Mary Kate wanted Aunt Mary to see the ducklings.

'They might not be there,' Mummy warned. 'They don't spend all their time by the bridge, you know.'

They were there, though. Mummy had brought some bread and Mary Kate dropped it over the rail into the stream. She gave Teddy to Aunt Mary to hold so that she wouldn't drop him, too.

'We *must* go now,' Mummy said, looking at her watch. 'We'll miss the bus if we don't.'

They hadn't been at the bus stop more than a minute or two when the bus came along.

'Toothbrush,' said Mary Kate, remembering.

'Too late now,' laughed Aunt Mary, helping Mary Kate on to the step.

'Can we go upstairs?' asked Mary Kate.

'Of course!' said Aunt Mary, so up they went.

'Good-bye, Granny,' shouted Mary Kate, looking out of the window and waving.

'Good-bye,' called Granny. 'See you on Saturday.'

There was no one else upstairs on the bus. Mary Kate and Teddy sat on one front seat and Mummy and Aunt Mary sat on the other. It was a long way to the hospital. After a little while Mary Kate went and sat on Mummy's lap and Teddy sat on Aunt Mary's lap and they all looked out of the wide window as the bus sped along the narrow lanes and through the quiet villages.

It was half past three when they reached the hospital. They had to go to Sister's office first and fill up a form.

'Where's Mr Smiley?' asked Mary Kate, when they came out.

'He'll come and see you presently,' Mummy told her.

23

A nurse in a blue uniform asked Mary Kate what her name was.

'Last bed on the right,' she said, when Mary Kate told her.

The ward seemed to be full of people. There were mothers and fathers and aunts and grandmothers and children everywhere.

'There's the pink nurse,' Mary Kate said. She was holding Mummy's hand very tightly and feeling rather shy because of all the strangers in the room.

The nurse in the pink uniform smiled when she saw Mary Kate. 'Hallo,' she said. 'You've brought your Teddy, then. I hope he behaves himself.'

'Oh, he will,' promised Mary Kate. 'He's a very *good* bear!'

Mummy took Mary Kate's dressing-gown and slippers out of the basket and put them on the bed. Then she took out the sponge bag. 'Oh, dear!' she said. 'We forgot the new toothbrush!'

'There might be a hospital shop,' Aunt Mary said. 'If not, there's a chemist just along the road. I remember seeing a blue glass jar in the window as we came by in the bus. Shall I go or will you?'

'I will,' said Mummy. 'I shan't be long.'

Off she went and Aunt Mary said, 'Come and have a ride on the rocking-horse, Mary Kate.'

24

While Mary Kate was having her ride the tea trolley was wheeled in. Little tables were pulled into the middle of the room and in a few minutes all the children were sitting round them, eating sandwiches and cake and drinking mugs of milk or orange juice.

Mary Kate had an egg sandwich and a jam sandwich and a piece of sponge cake. Then the tea things were cleared away.

Mary Kate was playing with the doll's house in the toy corner when Mummy came back with her new toothbrush.

'Sorry I've been so long,' Mummy said. 'I had some tea.'

'So did I,' said Mary Kate.

'Good gracious!' cried Mummy. 'That was quick!'

'It was only a little tea,' Mary Kate told her. 'I wanted some more but they took it away.'

'Well, if nobody minds,' said Aunt Mary, 'I think *I'd* like to go and have a little tea.'

When Aunt Mary came back from having her tea Mummy and Mary Kate were nowhere to be seen.

'They're in the bathroom,' said the nurse in the blue uniform, seeing Aunt Mary by Mary Kate's bed. Then Aunt Mary noticed that several of

the children were in their dressing-gowns and slippers.

Mummy was just lifting Mary Kate into the big, deep hospital bath when Aunt Mary opened the bathroom door.

'Stand with your back to the door,' said Aunt Mary to Mummy. 'I've brought Mary Kate a lovely nutty cake.'

'She can't eat cake in *here*!' exclaimed Mummy. 'Whatever will the nurses say?'

'They won't know,' said Aunt Mary, taking a hazel nut cookie out of a paper bag. 'She can eat it in the bath. The crumbs will go down with the water.'

Aunt Mary broke off a piece of cookie and popped it into Mary Kate's mouth.

'Cake in the bath today and ice cream in bed tomorrow,' she said.

Mary Kate laughed. She thought Aunt Mary was joking. Nobody had ever given her ice cream in bed.

When she was bathed and dried Mummy put her to bed. 'We must go now, darling,' she said. 'I'll come again tomorrow.'

As Aunt Mary kissed her she dropped a parcel in Mary Kate's lap.

Mary Kate was so busy opening it she hardly

27

had time to wave to Mummy and Aunt Mary as they went out of the door.

Inside the parcel was a paper bag and inside the paper bag was another parcel in yellow paper. Mary Kate pulled off the crepe paper and there was a pair of red and white striped pyjamas. They were just the right size for Teddy!

Ice Cream in Bed

When Mary Kate woke up she was surprised to see Daddy sitting by her bed.

'Hallo, Daddy,' she said. 'When did you come?'

'Just this minute,' said Daddy. 'You were fast asleep, so we waited for you to wake up. Mummy's here, too.'

Mummy was sitting the other side of the bed, by the window.

'How do you feel, darling?' she asked, smoothing Mary Kate's hair.

'All right,' said Mary Kate. 'My throat's sore.'

'We'll soon put that right,' said a cheerful voice and there, at the bottom of the bed, stood the pink nurse. She was holding a dish and a spoon.

29

Mummy took the dish and showed it to Mary Kate.

'Ice cream,' she said. 'Auntie said you'd be having ice cream in bed, didn't she?'

'Yes,' said Mary Kate, sitting up and reaching out her hand for the dish. 'Did you know Auntie gave me cake in the bath this afternoon, Daddy?'

'Did she?' laughed Daddy. 'Well, that's something *I've* never had! Come to think of it, I've never had ice cream in bed, either. It wasn't this afternoon you had the cake, though. It was yesterday.'

'Yesterday?' Mary Kate looked puzzled. 'I wasn't here yesterday.'

'Yes you were, pet,' Mummy told her. 'It's Friday today. Aunt Mary and I brought you here yesterday afternoon.'

'Friday?' said Mary Kate, slowly, spooning up her ice cream. 'Friday's the day Mr Smiley's going to make my nose better.'

'He's done it,' Daddy said. 'He did it this morning.'

Mary Kate put her hand up to her face to see if her nose was all right. It was.

'I don't remember,' she said in a puzzled voice.

Mummy smiled. 'You were asleep. We told you you wouldn't know anything about it, didn't we?'

'Was it magic?' asked Mary Kate, feeling her nose again.

'Sort of,' said Daddy. 'They give you something to make you sleep and when you wake up whatever has to be done has *been* done. I can't think of anything more magic than that, can you?'

'No,' agreed Mary Kate, finishing the ice cream. 'My throat has stopped being sore now.

Shall I stop having ear-aches, too, when I come home?'

'I hope so,' said Mummy. 'And stop snoring and getting stuffy colds.' She took the dish away and put it on the locker. Teddy was lying there, in his new pyjamas. Mummy gave him to Mary Kate.

The pink nurse came back to collect the dirty dishes. All the other children had had ice cream, too. They were all sitting up in their beds, looking as sleepy as Mary Kate.

'Five more minutes,' said the nurse. 'We want to get them settled for the night.'

'What night?' asked Mary Kate.

'*This* night,' said Daddy. 'It's nearly bed-time.'

Mary Kate looked so bewildered that Mummy had to laugh. 'You've been asleep *all* day,' she said. 'Never mind, darling. You'll be coming home tomorrow.'

Mummy and Daddy kissed her 'Good-night' and turned to go. At the last minute Daddy took something out of his pocket and threw it on the bed. It was a little parcel.

'Another parcel?' said the pink nurse, coming to look. 'What is it this time, I wonder?'

She helped Mary Kate to unfasten the brown

paper. Inside was a little doll, dressed like a nurse. Fixed to her arms by small rubber bands were two tiny baby dolls.

'Well!' exclaimed the pink nurse. 'Whatever will they think of next?'

She brought a bowl of warm water and took Mary Kate's sponge bag and hairbrush out of the locker.

'A little wash,' she said, 'and then I'll tidy your bed and you can go to sleep again. I expect you'll be going home tomorrow, won't you?'

'Yes,' said Mary Kate, shutting her eyes and holding up her face to be washed.

When Mummy and Daddy came to fetch Mary Kate the next morning they found her sitting up in bed, dressing Teddy.

'You're late,' she said. 'Some of the other children went straight after breakfast.'

'It's a long way to come,' Mummy said, taking Mary Kate's clothes out of her bag and putting the dressing-gown and slippers in.

When Mary Kate was dressed Daddy carried her out to the lift. Mummy followed them with the bag and Teddy. Mary Kate had put the little doll into Daddy's pocket so that the babies wouldn't catch cold.

'This isn't the way to the bus stop!' cried Mary

Kate, as Daddy turned the corner outside the hospital.

'We're not going by bus,' said Daddy. 'We've got a surprise for you. Here we are.'

He stopped by a side street. A little way along the street was a small green car and standing by the car was Uncle Ned! Auntie Dot was looking out of the back window and waving her hand.

'We started out at the crack of dawn to come and visit you in hospital,' said Auntie Dot, when Mary Kate was safely settled on her lap and Mummy had climbed into the back seat beside them. 'We didn't know you would be coming home so soon.'

'I had the snuffle taken out of my nose,' Mary Kate told her. 'Mr Smiley did it with magic while I was asleep.'

'Lovely,' smiled Auntie Dot, cuddling Mary Kate up close. 'And you're quite better now, are you?'

'She's supposed to rest for a day or two,' Mummy said. 'She must go to bed when we get home and no rushing about for a little while.'

'I don't want to go to bed,' grumbled Mary Kate. 'I want to see Auntie Dot and Uncle Ned.'

'So you shall, poppet,' promised Auntie Dot.

'We'll come and sit by your bed and talk to you.'

She looked across at Mummy and smiled. Mummy smiled back. It was a special kind of smile. Mary Kate knew at once what it meant.

'More secrets,' she thought, happily. 'I wonder what it is this time?'

It wasn't long before she knew. As soon as Uncle Ned turned his little green car into the drive Granny opened the front door.

'Everything's ready', she said. 'And lunch will be in about half an hour.'

'Good!' grinned Uncle Ned, rubbing his hands together. 'I'm rattling!'

Auntie Dot carried Mary Kate into the hall and through to the dining-room. Mummy came in with the bag. She warmed Mary Kate's pyjamas in front of the electric fire while Auntie Dot undressed her.

'Where's Auntie Mary?' asked Mary Kate.

'In her room, I expect,' said Mummy.

At that moment the door to the little room off the dining-room opened and Aunt Mary came out. 'Ready?' she asked.

'Yes,' said Auntie Dot, fastening the last button on Mary Kate's pyjama jacket.

'Right, then,' said Aunt Mary and turned back

into her room. Mummy picked Mary Kate up and followed Aunt Mary.

On top of Aunt Mary's bed was Mary Kate's blue eiderdown. Under the eiderdown was a big white bag.

'It's a sleeping bag,' Aunt Mary said. 'You put the pillow in the pocket at the top – see. Then you put yourself in the pocket at the bottom and we cover you up with the eiderdown. You can stay in bed down here in the daytime and we can take it in turns to come and talk to you. How's that?'

'Lovely,' sighed Mary Kate, snuggling down with Teddy. She was surprised to find that she really did feel rather tired.

'You have a little nap, pet,' Mummy said, smoothing her hair. 'You can have your lunch when you wake up.'

Everyone had finished lunch by the time Mary Kate woke up. Daddy and Uncle Ned were chatting by the shed in the garden, Granny and Auntie Dot were looking at the flowers, Aunt Mary was drying the washing-up and Mummy was making a pot of tea.

'Mummy,' called Mary Kate. Mummy didn't come, but Jacky the dog did. He put his paws on the side of the bed and wagged his tail and tried to lick Mary Kate's face.

'Go and fetch Mummy,' said Mary Kate. 'Tell her I want my lunch.'

Jacky put his head on one side and barked. Mummy heard him and came to see what was the matter.

'I'm hungry,' said Mary Kate.

'I'll bring you some soup,' Mummy told her. 'And there's a little mashed potato and mince. All right?'

Mary Kate nodded. 'Back in a minute, then,' Mummy said but it wasn't Mummy who came back with the tray. It was Aunt Mary. She brought her cup of tea in too, and drank it while Mary Kate ate her lunch.

As Aunt Mary took the tray away Uncle Ned appeared at the door. He was holding a glass dish high above his head and over his arm was a folded table napkin.

'Madam's dessert,' he said, bowing very low. 'They tell me that all the best people have their ice cream in bed these days.'

A Table for the Birds

It was Sunday morning. Mary Kate was already awake and playing with Og and Ben-Bun when Mummy went downstairs to make the tea. Mummy must have heard her talking to her toys, because when she came up with the tray she banged Mary Kate's door with her elbow and said, 'Come and have some tea, pet. I've brought your mug up.'

Mary Kate crawled carefully out of bed so as not to pull the blankets off Og and Ben-Bun and hurried out of her room and across the landing after Mummy.

There was a hump right in the middle of the big bed. It was Daddy. Only the top half of his face showed above the blankets and eiderdown. The pillows were pulled close round his head and his eyes were shut.

'Is Daddy asleep?' whispered Mary Kate, climbing quietly into the bed.

Mummy smiled. She was arranging the cups on the tray. She pulled the little trolley table close up to the bed, kicked off her furry slippers and slid in beside Mary Kate.

'Move over, pet,' she said. 'Give Daddy a shake and make him wake up.'

Mary Kate shook Daddy's shoulder under the blankets but he wouldn't open his eyes. She tickled the back of his neck. He grunted and wriggled away. When she poked him in the back with her foot he put his hand behind him quickly and caught her ankle and held it fast.

Mary Kate giggled and squirmed herself over so that she could look at Daddy's face. His eyes were still shut but he was smiling. 'Wake up,' she said, 'or Mummy will drink your tea and I'll eat your biscuits.'

As soon as he heard this, Daddy let go of Mary Kate's ankle and sat up. He rubbed his eyes and yawned and pretended to be surprised to see her.

'Is it morning already?' he asked. 'I've only been asleep five minutes.'

Mummy sugared his tea and stirred it for him and Mary Kate kept very still while she handed him the cup and saucer. Then Mummy put the plate of biscuits on Mary Kate's lap and gave her her blue-and-white striped mug. It was only half full and not too hot so she drank the milky tea straight away and gave the mug to Mummy again.

Daddy helped himself to two biscuits but just as he was putting one in his mouth a bit broke off and dropped on to the floor.

'Oh, dear!' whispered Daddy to Mary Kate. 'Must pick that up before Mummy sees it.'

He drank his tea and held out the cup to Mummy, saying, 'More, please.' As soon as Mummy had turned away to pour the tea, Daddy leaned over the side of the bed and picked up the bit of biscuit. He hid it behind one of the pretty jars on the dressing-table. Mummy pretended not to know.

When they had all had two cups of tea and the biscuit plate was empty, they snuggled under the blankets for five minutes and then Mummy said it was time she went down to start the breakfast.

Daddy was pretending to be asleep again, so Mary Kate wriggled up close to him and closed her eyes. After a few minutes she felt Daddy's big, warm hand fold round hers and give it a little squeeze.

'Don't make a sound, poppet,' he whispered in her ear. 'Just turn your head slowly and look towards the window.'

Mary Kate did as she was told. There, on the window-sill, sat a fat robin. The window was only open a little bit but the cheeky bird had found the way in without any fuss. Now he hopped down on to the dressing-table and stood with his head on one side, listening.

Daddy and Mary Kate kept very still and watched him. He began to hop across the dressing-table, looking all about him. He pecked at Mummy's pretty rings on the little china tree and poked his beak into the blue dish that held her hairpins. Then he found the bit of biscuit that Daddy had hidden behind the jar of hand cream. He started to eat it, pecking bits off and gobbling them up very fast. Then, suddenly, he stopped eating, picked up the last bit of biscuit in his beak and flew out of the window with it.

'He's gone to give Mrs Robin her breakfast in bed,' said Daddy.

Mary Kate laughed. 'Won't Mummy be surprised when we tell her?' she said. 'She always puts crumbs on the kitchen window-sill for the birds' breakfast. Perhaps she hasn't put any out this morning.'

Mummy hadn't put any crumbs out. 'It's a waste of time,' she said. 'Pipkin eats them. And if he doesn't want them, he sits so close to the window that the birds won't come. What we need is a proper bird-table.'

'I thought we had one,' said Daddy, helping himself to toast.

'We did,' Mummy told him, 'but it's broken. The top fell off in the gales last winter. That's when I started putting the crumbs on the window-sill. We didn't have Pussy Pipkin then, though.'

'Oh, well,' Daddy said, reaching for his special marmalade, 'if the post is still there, all we need is a new table. A bit of wood nailed on to the post will do, won't it?'

'No, it won't,' Mummy said. 'It's got to be a tray so the food won't blow off and so high that Pipkin can't jump up on to it. That means putting in a new post – a tall one – well away from the trees and fences.'

After breakfast Daddy went out into the garden. He said he was going to look for a place to put the bird-table. He was gone a long time and when Mary Kate went out to look for him he wasn't there. She was just going back to the house when she heard someone whistling in the little wood at the bottom of the garden. It was Daddy. He came through the gate carrying a long, rough post over his shoulder.

'This ought to do,' he said, lowering the post to the ground. 'I'll just saw a bit off the crooked end and dig a hole for it.'

By the time the post was sawn and the hole dug, it was twelve o'clock. Mary Kate could hear the church clock striking. Daddy heard it, too. He stopped digging and looked at his watch.

'My goodness me!' he cried. 'Is that the time? I promised your Granny I'd take her some brussels sprouts this morning. If I don't get a move on she'll have to have them for tea instead of lunch. Run and fetch a basket, Mary Kate, while I plant this post.'

When Mary Kate came back with the basket Daddy was trying to hold the post steady with one hand and shovel the earth into the hole with the other. 'Hold the post,' he said. Mary Kate held it as best she could and Daddy filled in the hole and stamped the earth down.

'That'll have to do for now,' he said, wiping his hands on his trousers. 'Come and help me pick the sprouts. Granny's having visitors for lunch today.'

'Yes, she is,' said Mummy's voice behind them and when Mary Kate and Daddy turned round they saw Mummy, with a colander in her hand. 'One o'clock lunch and you haven't even taken her the sprouts yet. You'll have to take her ours. They're all washed and ready for the pot. Put them in the basket and be off with you. I'll pick myself some more while you're gone. Have you finished the bird-table?'

'No,' said Daddy, tipping the clean sprouts into the basket. 'I've put the post in, though. It won't take long to make the tray.'

Mummy sniffed. 'Well, I hope you'll do it before the frosts come!' she said and hurried off to the vegetable plot.

Granny was very pleased to have the sprouts already washed.

'How thoughtful of you, dear,' she said. 'They're such fiddly things to do.'

Daddy looked at Mary Kate and Mary Kate looked at Daddy and they both looked at their feet and said nothing. They stayed talking to Granny and her visitors for so long that it was almost one o'clock before they started for home again.

'We're going to get into trouble for being late for lunch if we don't hurry,' Daddy said, as they went through the churchyard. 'As soon as we get into the field, you come up on my back and I'll run.'

Daddy ran all the way across the field and across the bridge and through the wood with Mary Kate bumping up and down on his back. Mummy was just taking the roast out of the oven when they arrived.

'Just in time,' panted Daddy, sliding Mary Kate on to the floor. 'I'll finish the bird-table after lunch.' He didn't, though. He went to sleep in his big chair by the fire. When he woke up it was almost tea-time.

'It's too dark to go outside and finish the bird-table now,' he said, peering out of the window at the low, grey sky.

'Just as well I finished it, then,' said Mummy, kneeling down in front of the glowing fire to toast the crumpets.

'*You* finished it?' cried Daddy, staring at her. 'This I must see!'

He went into the hall for his coat and then out of the front door and round the side of the house to the garden. Mary Kate followed him, pulling her coat round her as she went.

Round by the vegetable plot they went and there was the thick post that Daddy had put in before lunch. There were four deep round holes in the soft earth close to the post and on top of it was a seed-box.

'She stood on a chair to nail it on,' Daddy said, looking into the seed-box. He lifted Mary Kate up and carried her back to the house. 'There's no doubt about it, Mary Kate,' he said. 'Your mother is a very remarkable woman!'

'Yes,' said Mary Kate. She didn't know what it meant but she thought it must be nice because Daddy was laughing.

A Secret

Mary Kate had lost Mummy. It was silly, but she had. She stood on the top step of the house next door to Mrs Watson's wool shop and looked up the hill and down the hill, but Mummy wasn't there. Nor was Granny.

Mary Kate thought Granny had probably gone home, but she couldn't think what had happened to Mummy.

They had come out soon after lunch to do some shopping and bumped into Granny outside the Post Office. Granny said she was going to change her library book but she had one or two bits and pieces to buy so they all walked down the street together.

When they came to the Corner Store they saw that the windows had been decorated ready for

Christmas. They looked so gay and pretty that they all stopped to have a good look.

The Corner Store was the biggest shop in the village. It had two doors and three windows and there was an upstairs to it, just like a town store.

Mary Kate liked the Corner Store. She liked to run up the red-and-black tiled path that was the left-hand entrance, go through the door and behind the middle window and come out of the other door on to the black-and-white tiled path that was the right-hand entrance. She could only do that in the summer, of course, because in the winter the shop doors were shut to keep the cold out. A bell rang when they were opened and the assistants looked up to see who was coming in. They wouldn't have been very pleased to see Mary Kate come in and go out again without buying anything.

'I want some tape,' Granny said and went in through the left-hand door. Mary Kate hopped in behind her before she could shut it and stop the bell ringing.

It was cosy inside the shop and a bit muddly. They sold so many things. There were groceries and sweets and bread and cakes and boots and shoes and curtain materials and dresses and coats and all kinds of interesting knick-knacks.

Then Mummy came into the shop. 'I've seen something in the window that I want,' she said. 'Upstairs.' She made a funny face at Granny. Granny stared at her and then said 'Oh – yes. Of course! Come on, Mary Kate, let's go and buy some chocolate drops.'

Mary Kate wanted to go upstairs with Mummy but she wanted some chocolate drops, too, so she went with Granny to the sweet counter.

Granny bought some sweets for herself while she was about it and then she saw a display of Christmas Gifts and went to have a closer look at it.

Mary Kate followed her but they were all gifts for grown-ups so she wandered away after a bit. She thought she would go upstairs and see what Mummy was buying. She had only taken two steps when Granny pulled her back.

'Come and help me change my library book,' she said. 'Mummy will catch us up when she's finished here.'

'What's she gone to get?' asked Mary Kate.

'Little girls shouldn't ask questions,' said Granny. 'Not when it's nearly Christmas, anyway.'

She asked the assistant on the drapery counter to tell Mummy where she was going and then she and

Mary Kate went out of the shop and round the corner and up the hill.

The pavement was so narrow Mary Kate had to walk behind Granny, holding on to her coat.

The library was at the back of Mrs Watson's Wool Shop. It was just a big bookcase all along the wall. There was a smaller bookcase in the corner, behind a pile of cardboard boxes and bundles of wool. This was where the children's books were kept.

Mary Kate went to see if her favourite book was there. It was about a little white kitten with a black patch over one eye and was full of lovely pictures.

Mummy came into the shop. She didn't come right down to the library. She said, 'Hallo' to Mrs Watson and then she called out to Granny, 'I'm going to the Bun Shop to collect my order.'

'All right, dear,' said Granny, without looking up. 'I shan't be long.'

Mary Kate was only halfway through the book about the White Kitten, so she didn't go after Mummy. She knew she would have to come back past the Wool Shop because that was the way they went home.

Two or three people came into the shop. Mary Kate couldn't see the door from her corner behind

the boxes but she heard the bell ring several times. Mrs Watson was having a busy afternoon.

Mary Kate came to the end of her book. She got up from the box she had been sitting on and went to find Granny. Granny wasn't there. There were three other ladies choosing books but Granny had chosen hers and gone away. She hadn't seen Mary Kate anywhere about so she thought she must have gone to the Bun Shop with Mummy.

Mary Kate went quickly out into the street. Mrs Watson didn't see her, so she didn't know she had been there all by herself. She didn't *hear* her go, either, because somebody opened the door to come in just as Mary Kate reached it and she went out without having to make the bell ring.

She couldn't see Mummy or Granny anywhere. Even when she climbed the five steps outside the house next to the shop she still couldn't see them.

She came down from the steps and went slowly along the narrow path, down the hill to the Corner Store again. If she had gone *up* the hill she would have come, at last, to her own house, but she didn't think Mummy would go all the way home without her, so she went back to the village.

There was no one outside the Corner Store. The

Bun Shop was on the other side of the road and there was rather a lot of traffic at the corner.

Mary Kate walked along the front of the Corner Store, past the newspaper shop towards the Post Office. She thought she would try to cross the road near the Church. It was quieter at that end of the village because there weren't any shops there.

When Mary Kate came to the corner opposite the Church she hesitated. This was the lane where Granny lived. She knew Mummy wouldn't be there but she thought Granny might, so she ran quickly down to Granny's cottage. Round to the back door she ran, and banged and shook at the handle. The door wouldn't open, so Mary Kate knew Granny wasn't home yet.

Mary Kate ran back to the end of the lane. A bus was just coming up to the bus stop. She saw from the number on the front that this was the bus that would take her all the way home and put her down right opposite her own front door. There was a sixpence in her coat pocket. It had been there for ages because Mary Kate couldn't make up her mind what to do with it.

She put her hand into her pocket and felt the sixpence, but while she was wondering if the conductor would let her get on the bus by herself, he rang the bell and the bus moved off.

There was nothing coming either way so Mary Kate did her kerb drill very quickly and ran across. (She wasn't really certain which was left and which was right, so she looked both ways twice just to make sure.)

Down to the Bun Shop she ran, not stopping to look at anything on the way. Mummy wasn't there. The lady behind the counter knew Mary Kate but she didn't know she had lost Mummy. She thought Mummy was coming along behind somewhere.

She said, 'Hallo, Mary Kate. Tell Mummy her order's ready now.'

So Mummy's order hadn't been ready when she called for it. She would have to come back to the Bun Shop to collect it.

Mary Kate looked at the cakes and loaves in the Bun Shop window. They made her feel hungry. She remembered her sixpence. She was trying to make up her mind which cake she would buy when she noticed the shop next door.

It, too, had dressed its little bow window for Christmas. It was bright with tinsel and coloured paper and white with cotton-wool snow. In the middle of the bottom shelf was a Christmas crib. Mary Kate went to look at it.

Mummy came across the street from the hard-

ware shop and Granny came round the corner
from the Station Hill. A bus went by and a lady
with a pram squeezed Mary Kate against the
shop-front.

Granny and Mummy didn't see each other till
they were both by the Bun Shop.

'Sorry I kept you waiting,' puffed Granny. 'I
went to fetch my shoes from the menders. I met old
Mrs Cotterill and she kept me talking.'

'That's all right,' Mummy said. 'My order
wasn't ready. I've had to come back for it.'

'Well, let's have tea in the Bun Shop, then,'
Granny said. 'My treat.' She looked back at the
little bow window of the toy-shop. 'Come on, Mary
Kate. I'll buy you a doughnut,' she said.

Mary Kate followed Mummy and Granny into
the warm, spicy-nice shop.

She fingered the sixpence in her pocket and
smiled. She wouldn't have to buy a cake with it
after all.

She sat down at the table and looked at Mummy
and Granny. They were chattering and laughing
just as though nothing had happened.

They didn't know they had lost her. Granny
thought she had been with Mummy and Mummy
thought she had been with Granny.

Mary Kate helped herself to a jammy doughnut

and bit a big sugary piece out of it. She had had an adventure and she was going to keep it a secret.

A New Uncle

Uncle Jack was coming home. Granny had come bustling up the garden while Mummy and Daddy and Mary Kate were having breakfast, puffing and panting and waving a letter.

'Jack's in Paris!' she cried. 'He'll be here tomorrow.'

Mary Kate wanted to know who Jack was.

'Your other uncle,' Daddy told her. 'And don't talk with your mouth full.'

Mary Kate swallowed her cornflakes quickly and said she didn't remember Uncle Jack.

'You wouldn't,' said Daddy. 'He went off on his travels long before you were born.'

'He's been all round the world,' Granny said, proudly. 'Now he's coming home again.'

'Where does he live?' asked Mary Kate.

Daddy laughed. 'With Granny, of course,' he said. 'Where else?'

Then he stopped laughing and looked at Granny. So did Mummy.

'I know what you're thinking,' Granny said. 'He can't stay with me because I've turned the back bedroom into a bathroom. Well, he can have the attic. After all, it's where he and Ned slept when they were boys.'

'But it's full of junk!' cried Mummy.

'Yes,' said Granny. 'I came to ask you if you'd come and help me clear it out and spruce it up a bit.'

So Daddy and Mary Kate washed up while Granny and Mummy tidied and made the beds and then they all set off for Granny's house, taking Jacky the dog with them because they knew they would be away all day.

'What about lunch?' Mummy said as they came out of the churchyard into the village street.

'Soup and sandwiches,' said Daddy. 'This is an emergency.'

Granny went to send a telegram to Uncle Ned and telephone Aunt Mary while Mummy and Daddy and Mary Kate went to inspect the attic.

'Now don't get in the way, there's a good girl,'

Mummy said as Mary Kate followed her up the narrow stairs. 'We've a lot to do.'

So Mary Kate tried to make herself small and keep clear of Mummy and Daddy as they carried odds and ends of furniture down into the garden.

Some of the smaller things they put on the first landing for Mary Kate to take down while they were in the attic moving something else. They said she was a great help and saved their legs a lot.

Granny came back with some paint and brushes.

'Charlie Bean's bringing the ceiling stuff for me,' she told them. 'And he's coming with his cart later on to take away all the things I want to get rid of.'

'Good,' said Daddy. 'This garden is looking more like Charlie's yard every minute.'

Charlie Bean was the rag and bone man. He had a junk yard near the station.

When he came with his horse and cart Daddy helped him to load up all the things Granny didn't want.

By this time the attic was almost empty. 'Now we can clean it up a bit,' said Mummy 'and then we'll have lunch and Daddy can whitewash the ceiling.'

Granny made the sandwiches and heated the soup while Mummy and Daddy swept and dusted

in the attic to shift the worst of the dirt. Daddy had a duster tied over his head because he had forgotten to bring his garden cap. He looked like a pirate, Granny said.

In the middle of the afternoon Granny went out to do her Saturday shopping. She was going to do Mummy's too, because Mummy was helping Daddy do the ceiling.

Mary Kate didn't go with Granny. She stood by the attic door for a bit, watching Mummy and Daddy, and then she went down into the garden.

There was a man by the front gate. He was standing quite still looking at the house.

'Hallo,' he said. 'What's your name?'

'Mary Kate,' said Mary Kate. 'Granny isn't in. She's gone shopping.'

'She hasn't left you on your own, surely?' said the man.

'No,' said Mary Kate. 'Mummy and Daddy are here. They're whitewashing the ceiling.'

Just then Mummy came round the corner of the house to look for Mary Kate. She saw the man.

'Jack!' she cried and rushed down the path. The man put his arms round Mummy and lifted her right up in the air as though she had been a little girl.

'Put me down,' laughed Mummy. 'What are

63

you doing here, anyway? You're not supposed to come until tomorrow.'

'Couldn't wait,' said the man who was Uncle Jack. 'So I flew.'

Mummy looked worried. 'It'll upset Mother,' she said. 'You know how she likes to have everything just so. She's doing up your room. It'll spoil it for her if you turn up before it's ready.'

'What do you want me to do, then?' asked Uncle Jack. 'Hide?'

'Yes,' said Mummy, making up her mind. 'You do just that. Mary Kate, will you take Uncle Jack back to our house and keep him there out of Granny's way?'

'Does she know the way?' asked Uncle Jack, doubtfully, looking at Mary Kate.

'Of course she does,' Mummy told him. 'She came across the fields all by herself once when I was stuck in the loft. Stop wasting time and get going before Mother comes back.'

Uncle Jack still looked doubtful. 'Won't she wonder where the child is?' he asked.

Mummy had a bright idea. 'I'll fetch Jacky,' she said. 'I'll tell Mother she's taken the dog for a walk and she'll think they've gone up to the Green.'

The Green was a fenced-off field at the end of the

lane. There were swings there and a see-saw. It was quite a safe place for Mary Kate to go on her own.

So Mary Kate set off with Jacky and Uncle Jack to take the short cut home. She felt very grown-up and important as she led the way through the churchyard.

Uncle Jack managed the stiff latch on the gate in the wall quite easily.

'It needs wiggling,' he said. 'It's wonky.'

'How did you know?' asked Mary Kate, surprised.

Uncle Jack laughed. 'I was wiggling this latch before you were born or thought of,' he told her. 'Which way now?'

'Down here,' said Mary Kate, leading him along the narrow alley between the hedge and the high brick wall. When they reached the kissing-gate she stopped. 'You go first,' she said. 'Jacky always gets in a muddle with this gate.'

'Let him off the lead then,' said Uncle Jack. Then he went through the gate. 'Now you've got to pay me a forfeit,' he said.

'That's what Daddy says,' laughed Mary Kate and she gave her new uncle a kiss to make him open the gate.

Jacky was already a long way down the footpath that led to the bridge. Uncle Jack and Mary Kate hurried after him.

They stopped on the bridge to look at the stream. 'This is where we feed the ducks,' said Mary Kate. She was rather sorry the ducks weren't there for Uncle Jack to see.

'I know,' said Uncle Jack, throwing a pebble

into the water. 'I used to come here when I was a boy, with your Uncle Ned. Aunt Mary too, and your mother.'

It seemed rather odd to Mary Kate to think of Uncle Jack and Uncle Ned and Mummy and Aunt Mary being children and feeding the ducks just as she did. She thought of them all in Granny's cottage – the two little girls in the back bedroom that was now the bathroom and the two boys in the attic. What a lot of room they must have taken up in Granny's kitchen.

Jacky was barking outside the back door by the time Uncle Jack and Mary Kate reached the gate at the bottom of the garden.

'So this is where you live, is it?' said Uncle Jack. 'Plenty of room for me, is there?'

'Oh, yes,' said Mary Kate. 'You can have Auntie Mary's room.'

She showed Uncle Jack where the tea-things were and fetched the cake tin out of the larder because he said he was peckish.

By the time Mummy arrived Mary Kate and her new uncle were chatting and laughing as though they had known one another for years.

'I telephoned Mary,' Mummy said. 'She's coming down with Ned and Dot tomorrow. We're having a party.'

Uncle Jack went to Granny's house on Sunday morning as though he had just arrived and in the afternoon Mummy and Daddy and Mary Kate went across and pretended to be surprised to see him.

It was a *wonderful* party. Granny was so pleased to have all her family at home again.

Of course, when Uncle Jack had really settled in they told Granny how he had arrived a day too soon, but for quite a while only Mummy and Daddy and Aunt Mary knew how Mary Kate had taken her new uncle home and hidden him so that he wouldn't spoil Granny's surprise.

The Wedding

It was the very middle of the night. Mary Kate was fast asleep with Teddy in his new pyjamas lying sideways on the pillow above her head. Mummy had put him there when she went to bed so he wouldn't sit on Mary Kate's face in the night.

Down in the dining-room the wall clock began to chime. Three o'clock, it said in its sweet, silvery voice but nobody heard it. Nobody was awake.

Upstairs on Mummy's bedside table the little alarm clock was busily ticking away the minutes. As soon as the dining-room clock stopped chiming, the whirring wake-up bell in the bedroom began to ring.

Mummy heard it and put out her hand to stop the noise. Daddy heard it and pulled the blankets over his head. Mary Kate didn't hear it. Her bed-room door was shut and so was Mummy's.

It was Mummy who woke Mary Kate, a little while later. She stood by the bed with a mug of milky tea in her hand, all dressed up to go out except for her coat.

'Wake up, pet,' she said. 'Drink up this tea and eat a biscuit or two and then I'll get you dressed.'

Mary Kate sat up and rubbed her eyes. 'Why have you got your hat on?' she said – and then she remembered.

This was the day Mummy's Cousin Ruth was getting married and Mary Kate was going to be a bridesmaid. Mummy had told her she would have to wake up before it was light because the wedding was going to be early and they had a long way to go.

When Mary Kate had had her tea and biscuits she went to the bathroom to wash. Daddy was there to help her so that Mummy wouldn't get her best dress splashed. Daddy was still in his dressing-gown. He said *he* only needed ten minutes to go from bed to bus stop.

'No use going to the bus stop this morning,' Mummy told him. 'The buses aren't running yet.'

It was just after four o'clock when they left the house. They closed the front door quietly and crept down the steps to the road. Daddy put the key through Mrs Next-Door's letterbox so that she could go in and look after Jacky and Pussy Pipkin when she woke up. It was very strange to be walking to the station in the dark, still, early morning. It wasn't a bit like being out late at night.

Here and there a street lamp shone softly but there were no lights to be seen anywhere in the silent houses. Not a car, not a bus, not a bicycle went by as they walked through the empty village. It seemed to Mary Kate that she and Mummy and Daddy were the only people awake in all the world.

Then they saw Granny and Uncle Jack. They came hurrying round the corner from the lane opposite the Church. Mummy and Daddy and Mary Kate stopped by the Post Office and waited for them.

'Thought we'd save you the trip to fetch us,' Granny said as soon as she was near enough for them to hear her whisper. She took Mary Kate's hand and they all walked, whispering, to the station at the bottom of the hill.

The station was just as quiet and empty as the village. There was no one in the booking hall, no one in the waiting room and no one on the platform. The small yellow lights were a long way apart and not very bright. They made the dark places behind them seem darker still. It was so gloomy and different from the station in the day-time that Mary Kate had a funny feeling that it wasn't really her own village station at all.

A man in a peaked cap came out of an inner office and looked at them. He had a mug of tea in his hand and he was yawning. He opened the shutters on the booking office window and Daddy bought the tickets to London.

They heard the train coming long before they saw it. Then it swept round the curve of the line and into the station like a long, black caterpillar patterned all down its body with squares of yellow light.

There weren't many passengers on it and those that were sat huddled up in the corner seats, most of them half-asleep.

Mummy and Daddy and Granny and Uncle Jack settled themselves comfortably in corner seats and Mary Kate sat close to Granny and leaned her head against her.

'If I were you, Mary Kate,' Granny said, 'I should lie down on the seat and have a little nap. We don't want you falling asleep in the church, do we?'

Mary Kate didn't think she wanted a nap but she stretched herself out on the seat beside

Granny and closed her eyes. Mummy took a cardigan out of one of the bags and covered her up with it.

The guard blew his whistle, the train began to move – and long before they reached the next station Mary Kate was asleep.

She slept all the way to London. Mummy had to shake her and rub her legs and lift her down on to the platform. Even then she didn't wake up properly. Daddy carried her across the big, busy station, through the brightly lighted ticket hall to the chilly yard, and they took a taxi to Auntie Dot's house.

It was nearly six o'clock and the grey morning light was making the street lamps look pale. Milk floats were rattling along the quiet streets and the sleepy houses were being woken up, their curtains drawn back, their bedroom windows opened.

Mary Kate was wide awake by the time they reached Auntie Dot's house. Uncle Ned opened the door to them and shouted 'They're here!' to Auntie Dot, who was in the kitchen.

'Right!' called Auntie Dot. 'I'll make the tea.'

'Good,' said Granny. 'That's what I like to hear,' and she and Mummy and Mary Kate took off their outdoor things and put them in Auntie

Dot's front room. Daddy and Uncle Jack put their things on the hall-stand and went into the dining-room to warm their hands by the fire.

Mary Kate ate an *enormous* breakfast. When she finished her third piece of toast Auntie Dot said she'd better not have any more or her new dress wouldn't fit her.

'Am I going to put it on now?' asked Mary Kate.

'No,' said Mummy. 'We're all going to go upstairs and put on our wedding clothes now because we're only guests, but *you* don't change till you get to Cousin Ruth's house. You're special. You're a bridesmaid.'

Mummy and Granny had come up to London weeks ago to buy their wedding clothes. They had left them at Auntie Dot's house so they wouldn't get grubby and crumpled on the train journey. Aunt Mary had come down to the village to look after Mary Kate. She was going to be a bridesmaid, too. She had taken Mary Kate to the village church and told her exactly what was going to happen at Cousin Ruth's wedding.

When Mummy and Granny and Auntie Dot came downstairs again they looked very beautiful. They had pretty flowery hats on and they smelled lovely. Uncle Ned and Uncle Jack and Daddy looked rather splendid, too, in their striped trousers and tall hats.

At eight o'clock the hired car came to take them to Cousin Ruth's house. Though it was still so early in the morning, the house seemed to be full of people, all wearing new clothes.

Cousin Ruth was nowhere to be seen but Great-Aunt Jo came to the top of the stairs and called to Mary Kate to come up.

'In the back bedroom, darling,' she said, giving Mary Kate a little push. 'Dolly will see to you. I must finish dressing.'

There was a good deal of chatter and laughter coming from the back bedroom. Great-Aunt Jo opened the door and Mary Kate went in.

'Here she is!' said several people at once and then Aunt Mary was standing in front of her, looking like a princess in a long blue gown with pink roses at the hem.

There were eight bridesmaids altogether, three more tall ones in gowns just like Aunt Mary's and three more little girls wearing dresses like the one put out on the bed for Mary Kate. It was pink and frilly and all over ribbons and lace. Mary Kate thought it was lovely.

There seemed to be hands everywhere, unbuttoning her, pulling her skirt over her head, taking off her shoes and socks. Somebody wiped her hands and face with a warm wet sponge. It was the third time she had been washed that day – once at home and once at Auntie Dot's and now again at Cousin Ruth's!

Now she was being put into the pink frilly dress. Someone was straightening her new white socks and someone else was fastening one of her new white shoes. Cousin Ruth's sister, Dolly, began to brush Mary Kate's hair and then Aunt Mary fixed a little wreath of flowers on her head.

'There!' she said. 'Now we're all ready!' She pushed Mary Kate towards the door, saying, 'Come and stand at the top of the stairs for a minute so Mummy can see you before she goes.'

'Where's she going?' asked Mary Kate in surprise.

'To the church,' Aunt Mary told her. 'The cars are here already. We'll be going ourselves in a minute or two.'

Mummy and Granny and Auntie Dot waved and smiled at Mary Kate as they went out of the front door. They were wearing flowers. Daddy and Uncle Ned and Uncle Jack had white carnations in their buttonholes.

There were four big shining cars in the road outside the house. They all had white ribbons on and looked very grand.

Soon it was Mary Kate's turn to go in one of the cars. She went with Aunt Mary and Cousin Dolly and one of the other little bridesmaids.

The church was full of people and flowers. The organ was playing softly and the morning sun shone through the tall windows in broken bits of colour. It was all so strange and beautiful that Mary Kate quite forgot to be nervous.

77

When the service was over, they all went outside and stood on the steps in the pale spring sunshine to have their pictures taken. Then, suddenly, it was raining confetti and rose petals and rice and everyone was laughing, and Cousin Ruth and the tall bridesmaids were squealing and running for the cars.

Uncle Ned lifted Mary Kate up so that she wouldn't be crushed.

'Where are we going now?' she asked.

'To the Royal Hotel for breakfast,' said Uncle Ned.

'We've *had* breakfast!' cried Mary Kate. 'We had it at *your* house.'

'This is the *wedding* breakfast,' Uncle Ned told her. 'There'll be a lot of it and it'll last a long time, so make the most of it, Mary Kate. It'll probably have to do us for lunch and tea as well!'